خالی
Empty and Me

A Tale of Friendship and Loss

Azam Mahdavi اعظم مهدوی
illustrated by Maryam Tahmasebi تصویرگری مریم طهماسبی
translated by Parisa Saranj ترجمه پریسا سارنج

LEE & LOW BOOKS

New York

Originally published under the title of *Khali*
Copyright © 2021 by Houpaa Books, Tehran, Iran

Text © 2021 by Azam Mahdavi
Illustrations © 2021 by Maryam Tahmasebi
Translation by Parisa Saranj © 2023 by Lee & Low Books Inc.

LEE & LOW BOOKS INC., 95 Madison Avenue, New York, NY 10016 | leeandlow.com

English-Persian edition edited by Stephanie Frescas Macías
Book design by Elliane Mellet
Book production by The Kids at Our House
The text is set in Archer Semibold
The illustrations are rendered digitally

Manufactured in China by RR Donnelley
1 3 5 7 9 10 8 6 4 2
First Edition

MIX
Paper | Supporting
responsible forestry
FSC® C144853

Cataloging-in-Publication Data at Library of Congress

HC ISBN: 978-1-64379-622-2 EBK ISBN: 978-1-64379-623-9

این آخرین عکس من و مامان است
و آخرین گلی که با هم کاشتیم...

This is the last picture of Mom and me
and the last pot we planted together.

بعدش مامان مُرد و خالی جایش را گرفت.

Then, Mom died, and Empty took her place.

خالی تنها دوست من بود...

Empty was my only friend.

او همیشه با من بود...

Empty was always with me.

همه‌جا با من بود.

Empty went with me everywhere.

خالی من را از مدرسه به خانه می‌برد...

Empty picked me up from school.

و در خانه کنارم بود، خیلی نزدیک...

At home, Empty stayed very close to me.

حتی وقتی با بابا به شهربازی رفتیم.

Even when Dad and I went to the amusement park.

تا اینکه یک روز...

آخرین گلدانی که با مامان کاشته بودیم گل داد!

Until one day, the last pot
Mom and I planted together bloomed.

و من یکی از گل‌هایش را به خالی هدیه دادم.

I gave one of the flowers to Empty.

یک روز دیگر، بچه‌گربه‌ی تنهایی را دیدم...

Another day, I found a lonely kitten.

و با خالی نجاتش دادیم...

Empty and I rescued it.

گربه با ما دوست شد.

The kitten became our friend.

آن شب، بابا برای من و
خالی و گربه کتاب خواند.

That night, Dad read me, Empty,
and the kitten a bedtime story.

روز بعد، یکی از دوست‌های مدرسه‌ام خالی را
دید و پشتش قایم شد.

The next day, one of my school friends
saw Empty and played with us.

آن شب، همه دور هم شام خوردیم.

That evening, Empty, the kitten,
Dad, and I had dinner together.

و فردایش یک نمایش خنده‌دار تماشا کردیم.

The day after that, we saw a funny play.

این آخرین عکسمان است...
و اولین گلی که با هم کاشتیم.

This is the last picture of us
and the first pot we planted together.

Azam Mahdavi is a freelance author, artist, translator, and graphic designer based in Tehran. She has published dozens of books for children and young adults in Iran, which have received awards in different national festivals, such as the Institute for the Intellectual Development of Children and Young Adults Festival. *Empty and Me* is her first book to be published in the U.S. You can follow her on Instagram at @azamm_mahdavi.

"I am a small part of this big, beautiful world. I have always loved reading and telling stories. Sometimes, my stories turn out nicely and I share them with others. That's how my stories come to life. *Empty and Me* is one of those stories."

Maryam Tahmasebi is a freelance illustrator and designer based in Tehran, with a degree in graphic design from the University of Tehran. She's illustrated six books published in Iran. *Empty and Me* is also the first book she's illustrated to be published in the U.S. You can find more of her work and information about her at maryamtahmasebi.org.

"I was born in the spring of 1993 in Tehran. I have always been fascinated by lines, colors, and shapes playing on paper. What I enjoy the most is watching carefree children sit around and read a book I am a part of. Traveling into the world of a book is very exciting for me. I hope it is for you too."

Parisa Saranj was born in Isfahan, Iran. Her writings and translations have appeared in several publications, including *Ms. Magazine*, *Two Lines*, and *Consequence*. She lives in Baltimore with her cat, Abnabat Choobi, which means "lollipop" in Persian. You can find both of them on social media at @PSaranj.

"As far as I remember, I wanted to become a writer to tell the stories of people I love. It wasn't until I learned English that I realized I could share their stories with the world. When I see the reader's reaction to my translations, I know we have the same dreams and worries everywhere. This is what makes us human."